Pajama Day!

Written by Margaret McNamara
Illustrated by Mike Gordon

Ready-to-Read

Simon Spotlight
New York London Toronto Sydney New Delhi

SIMON SPOTLIGHT
An imprint of Simon & Schuster Children's Publishing Division
1230 Avenue of the Americas, New York, New York 10020
This Simon Spotlight edition December 2020

For information about special discounts for bulk purchases, please contact Simon & Schuster
Special Sales at 1-866-506-1949 or business@simonandschuster.com.
Manufactured in the United States of America 1020 LAK
2 4 6 8 10 9 7 5 3 1
ISBN 978-1-5344-6828-3 (hc)
ISBN 978-1-5344-6827-6 (pbk)
ISBN 978-1-5344-6829-0 (eBook)

Emma and her dad
were walking to school.
Suddenly, Emma gasped.
She remembered something.

“Today is Pajama Day!”
she said.
“Great!” her dad said.

"I have to wear pajamas,"
Emma told him.
"If I do not wear pajamas,
people will think I have
no school spirit!"

“Your skirt looks like
pajamas,” her dad said.
“No, it does not!”
said Emma.

"Maybe not,"
her dad said.
"I will go get your
dinosaur pajamas."
"Hurry, please!" said Emma.

In the classroom everybody was wearing pajamas.

Michael wore puppy pajamas.

Katie wore a fancy nightgown.

Eigen wore footie pajamas.

Mrs. Connor wore
striped pajamas,
a bathrobe, and fuzzy slippers!

Emma felt terrible.
She looked at the clock
all morning.
Her dad did not come
back with pajamas.

“You can borrow my robe,”
said Mrs. Connor.

Emma really wanted
her dinosaur pajamas.
“No, thank you,” she said.

The class worked on
Pajama Day cheers.
The cheers were about
school spirit.

Mrs. Connor said,
"Robin Hill!"
The class said,
"Yes, we will!"

Mrs. Connor said,
“Hey! Hey!”

The class said,
"Pajama Day!"

At lunchtime
the kids ate breakfast
food instead of lunch food.

In the afternoon
they learned about animals
that sleep during the day.

Finally, it was time for
the Pajama Day rally.
All the teachers and students
were wearing pajamas.

They looked so happy!
"I am too sad to cheer,"
said Emma.

Just then,
Emma's dad walked in.
He was wearing his pajamas!

"Here are your dinosaur pajamas," he said.

"Thank you, Dad!"
said Emma.
"Now we both have
school spirit!"

It was time to cheer.
"Hey! Hey!"
said the teachers.